This book belongs to:

_____

DISNEY

Tuck-in Tales

Stories About Helping

DISNEY
Tuck-in Tales

**Stories About
Helping**

SCHOLASTIC INC.

New York Toronto London Auckland Sydney
Mexico City New Delhi Hong Kong Buenos Aires

Published by Scholastic Inc.,
90 Old Sherman Turnpike, Danbury, Connecticut 06816.

ISBN 0-7172-7796-8

Printed in the U.S.A.
First printing, May 2005

Designed by North Woods Design Group

CONTENTS

Adapted by Irene Trimble

Illustrated by Jeff Albrecht Studios

One day, Buzz Lightyear, Mira, Booster, and XR were stuck working on intergalactic speed-trap duty.

"Traffic looks like it's bumper to bumper," sighed Mira as she watched the crawling spacecraft.

Suddenly a large alien ship zoomed by. *VRROOM!*

"Strap in, team!" Buzz ordered, as they took off after the speeding ship. "Looks like we got ourselves a real hotshot!"

"Attention!" Mira announced. "We are the Space Rangers! Pull over immediately!" But the ship didn't stop. And it was heading right for the moon of San de Soleil!

"Blast!" cried Buzz. "If it keeps moving that fast, it's going to make one big explosion!" He fired off magnetic restraining cables to try to slow down the alien ship. The cables weren't strong enough.

As the cables broke off, Buzz and the crew helplessly watched the moon blast apart with a giant *KABOOM!*

"That ship didn't even slow down!" exclaimed Buzz. "At its current rate of speed, it'll crash into the sun and cause a supernova that could destroy the entire universe!"

"According to my calculations, that'll be in about one hour," added XR.

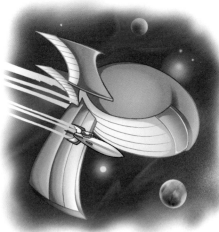

"We've got to stop that ship!" declared Buzz. He steered his ship right next to the alien craft and activated the magna-locks. "We'll board it through the air locks, Rangers."

But when the crew entered the ship, they found no one there.

"Hello-o-o, is anybody home?" Booster's voice echoed.

"Maybe the crew abandoned ship," said XR.

Suddenly a little robot carrying a feather duster scooted across the floor.

"Care-bot is online! Please wipe your feet! No space dust allowed! No dust, no dust, no dust!" the robot shouted. Then it scooted back into the darkness.

"Uh, what was that?" asked XR.

Before anyone could answer, another Care-bot came back with a can of air freshener. "No space germs allowed!" it shouted as it sprayed a puff of deodorizing mist at Buzz, who then grabbed the Care-bot by its neck.

"Who's in charge of the ship?" Buzz demanded. "And where's your crew?"

"Care-bot online!" shouted the Care-bot. "Cleanliness is top priority!"

"As it should be," answered Buzz. He let the Care-bot go.

"This robot butler is no help," he said to his crew. "Let's go to the bridge and see if we can stop this ship ourselves."

Buzz sat at the ship's controls. "They haven't made a spaceship I can't fly," he said confidently. Buzz flipped a switch, causing a light to blink on and off.

"Uh, Buzz, I think that's the turn signal," said XR.

Buzz pushed another switch. A little red ring popped out of the control panel. "Oh, a cup holder!" said Booster.

"Blast!" cried Buzz. "Let's just blow up this ship and get on with our day!"

Buzz and his Space Rangers carefully armed four bombs.

"T minus 60 seconds to detonation," said Mira.

"Okay, Rangers, time to exit the ship before it blows!" announced Buzz.

But as they arrived at the air lock, the Space Rangers discovered that the magna-locks weren't working. And their ship had taken off without them!

"Oh no!" cried Booster. "There goes our ride!"

"T minus two seconds to detonation," announced Mira.

Buzz stood tall and gave a final salute. "At least the explosion will keep this ship from crashing into the sun and causing even more damage!"

The Space Rangers were ready for the big KABLOOIE, when they heard, "Care-bot is online! We must not leave our explosive devices around willy-nilly!"

"Look," said Buzz, "the Care-bot has defused the bombs . . . and neatly, too!"

"Hey, hey, my cyber-brother," XR said to the little Care-bot. "You saved us!"

"Care-bot is online!" the Care-bot said. "Messy visitors! Messy visitors!"

"We still have to find a way to stop this ship!" Buzz reminded his crew, as they watched the Care-bot scurry away.

"Hmmm," said Booster. "We've tried slowing it down and blowing it up. Maybe we can fix the engine and shut it off!"

"That's it!" exclaimed Buzz. "We must find the power source! Get to it, rookie!" he told Booster.

Booster made his way to the lowest level of the ship. He thought he heard other Care-bots behind a closed door, so he slowly opened the door to peek inside.

Just as Booster walked through the doorway, he was hit in the face with a freeze ray! "Oh no!" yelled Booster over his radio.

Buzz, Mira, and XR followed Booster's radio signal and found him and the crew of the alien ship—frozen in huge blocks of ice.

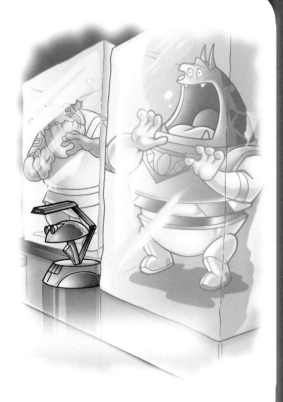

"This is what we do to all messy visitors!" announced a Care-bot. "Care-bot online!"

"I should have known," Buzz shouted to XR. "The butler did it!"

"C'mon, Buzz!" urged XR, as the Care-bots froze Mira. "It's us against a bunch of neat freaks!"

"Right you are, XR!" said Buzz, as he blasted away with his laser. "Buzz Lightyear is online!"

Thinking fast,
Buzz opened a
garbage chute
that sucked the
Care-bots out into
space. "I'm a bad
odor. And you, my
friends, are out of
lemon-fresh scent!"

Buzz rushed to melt Mira, Booster, and the alien crew with his
laser. "Now let's stop this ship!" he said to an alien crew member.

"It's simple," said the
alien, as he popped
the cup holder from
the control panel.
"This is the manual
overdrive system."
He slowed down the
ship just seconds before
it would have hit
the sun.

"Thank you for saving us," said the sloppy alien with a burp. "I programmed the Care-bots to clean up all messes, but they thought we were part of the mess, too."

"Just doing our job," commented Mira.

"And speaking of doing our job," added Buzz, "your ship was exceeding the galactic speed limit. I'm afraid I'm going to have to give you a ticket."

Disney's THE LION KING

SIMBA'S · PRIDE

The Outback Adventure

Written by Barbara Bazaldua

Illustrated by Alvin S. White Studio

"I'm too pooped to walk another inch," Pumbaa told Timon as they hiked through the Australian outback.

"Me, too," Timon agreed. He sat down on a large, oval-shaped greenish rock and began to rub his tired, hot feet.

Suddenly the stone he was sitting on jerked so hard that Timon fell off. "Pumbaa, this rock just rolled—by itself!" Timon yelped, staring at the stone. As he watched, huge cracks appeared. A sharp yellow beak poked out, followed by a tiny head and a long, scrawny neck. In a few minutes, a baby emu emerged.

"Timon, you were sitting on an egg! You hatched an emu!" Pumbaa laughed.

The little chick saw Timon and squeaked happily. It
stumbled over and rubbed against him. "Look, Timon,"
Pumbaa chuckled. "The little guy thinks you're his mama."

"Shoo! Go away! Move it! I'm not your mother!" Timon
shouted. He backed away, but the baby emu followed him.
It opened and shut its beak, squeaking loudly.

"He's hungry," Pumbaa said. "Let's find him some bugs
to eat."

Soon the little emu was gulping down grubs and squawking for more. Timon scooped up a handful of beetles. The baby bird swallowed them and squeaked again. Timon tossed ants into the little bird's mouth like popcorn. But still, the little bird squawked.

"Whoever said eating like a bird meant not eating much sure didn't know what he was talking about," Timon gasped as he and Pumbaa ran back and forth with bugs for the baby bird. "I don't think we can keep this up for long."

"Maybe we should try to find his real mom," Pumbaa said.

So the two friends set off with the little bird to look for his mother. Soon they came to a eucalyptus grove. "Birds like trees," Pumbaa said. "Maybe the mama emu is here."

The trio hurried into the grove of trees and looked around. The little bird squawked loudly for more to eat. "Be quiet!" a voice yelled suddenly from high in the trees. Timon and Pumbaa looked up and saw a koala yawning above them. The koala rubbed its eyes. "Tell that noisy little squawker to be quiet," the koala snapped. "He woke me up."

"We're sorry," Timon said. "We're just looking for this little guy's mama. Have you seen her?"

"No," the koala answered. "I'm napping. Or at least I *was* napping. Now scram, so I can get some rest." The koala began throwing sticks and leaves at Timon, Pumbaa, and the little emu. A large stick fell near Timon.

"Wow! Great walking stick," he said. He picked it up and ran out of the grove as more sticks and leaves rained down.

"That koala wasn't much help at all," Pumbaa said, as he walked on.

"Well, koalas sleep during the day, you know," Timon explained. "And Mr. Loud Beak did wake him up, after all."

All day they trudged, looking everywhere for a flock of emus. They climbed up rolling hills and clambered down rocky ridges. They walked around large bushes and crawled through tall grass. But they didn't see a flock of emus anywhere they looked.

At last, they came to a wide green river. "Water!" Timon shouted. "Just what my feet need. My toes feel like french fries." He waded into the river's shallow edge.

"But how are we going to get across, Timon?" Pumbaa asked. "We can't swim."

Suddenly an enormous crocodile rose from the water. With a shriek, Timon jumped back to the bank. The crocodile grinned at him. "Don't be afraid," he said, smiling slyly. "I heard you wondering how to cross the river. I'll carry you on my back."

"Yeah, and then you'll gobble us up," Timon answered.

"No, I won't." The crocodile smiled wider. "I'm not hungry— yet. Just climb on. There's room inside—er, I mean on board— for you all."

But Timon was still suspicious, and he whispered to Pumbaa, "Watch every move this guy makes. I don't trust him."

"Oh, Timon. He's just trying to help," Pumbaa argued. "Besides, he has such a nice big smile. He *must* be friendly."

So Timon, Pumbaa, and the little bird climbed onto the crocodile's back and sat down, and the crocodile swam across the river.

But just as they were about to reach the opposite bank, the crocodile twisted his head around and snapped at them. "Fooled you," he grinned.

"Grab the bird and jump to the bank," Timon shouted. "I'll take care of Mr. Scale Breath."

As Pumbaa and the little emu leaped ashore, Timon jammed his walking stick between the crocodile's jaws and wedged them open. Then he jumped to the bank, too.

Timon, Pumbaa, and the little bird ran as fast as they could. When the river was far behind them, they stopped to rest. They were very hot and tired.

"What do we do now?" Pumbaa asked. "We've looked everywhere. But we still haven't found this baby's mother."

As Timon and Pumbaa thought about their predicament, a mama kangaroo hopped by. She was peering around bushes and behind rocks. "Joey! Oh, Joey, where are you?" the kangaroo called.

"Look, Timon," Pumbaa said. "A mama kangaroo."

"Pumbaa, we're looking for a mama emu, not a mama kangaroo," Timon answered.

"But Timon—kangaroos have pockets," Pumbaa explained. "Maybe the little bird could climb inside and . . ."

Timon shook his head. "Pumbaa, that idea is so dumb it's—" Then he got the idea himself. Timon snapped his fingers. "Pumbaa, I have an idea!" he shouted. "Maybe the kangaroo would give the baby a ride to its mother. She can hop much farther and faster than we can walk."

"That's what I thought," Pumbaa answered. But Timon was already running over to speak with the kangaroo.

The sun was in the kangaroo's eyes, and she couldn't see very well. When she saw Timon, she thought he was her little kangaroo. "Oh, Joey, you naughty little kangaroo!" she cried as she picked up Timon. "I've been looking everywhere for you!"

"I'm not Joey, I'm Timon and—" Before Timon could say another word, the mama kangaroo popped him into her pouch. "We're going back to the rest of the kangaroos right now," she said, and off she bounded in great leaps.

"Puuuuuumbaa!" Timon shrieked as he bounced up. "*Ooof!*" He groaned as he jounced down. "Saaaave! Ugh! Meeee! *Ooof!*"

Pumbaa slung the little emu onto his back and dashed after Timon and the kangaroo. They arrived just as Timon crawled from the mama kangaroo's pouch and flopped to the ground. A little kangaroo ran up. "Who's this Mama?" he asked, looking at Timon. "Oh, my goodness!" the mama kangaroo exclaimed. "I thought it was you, Joey. I thought I was bringing you back, but you were already here."

"I tried to tell you," Timon spluttered. "But it's very hard to talk when you're being bounced around like a beach ball."

"I'm so sorry," the mama kangaroo said. "Is there anything I can do to help you now? Would you like a ride back?"

"Oh no, thank you. I'll just walk," Timon answered quickly.

"But Timon—maybe there *is* something she could do," Pumbaa spoke up. He put the baby emu in front of the mama kangaroo. "We've been trying all day to help this little bird find his mama," he told the kangaroo. "You travel so fast and so far, perhaps you could take him to his flock."

"Why, I saw a flock of emus not far from here," the mama kangaroo answered. "I'll take the little bird to them. His mama will be there, I'm sure."

"Thank you," Timon said, as the kangaroo lifted the little bird into her pouch. Joey climbed in, too.

"Well, good-bye, little guy." Timon and Pumbaa patted the grateful baby emu on the head. It peeped happily and waved a stubby wing at them as it bounced away in the mama kangaroo's pouch.

Timon and Pumbaa watched until the kangaroo was out of sight. Then they grinned at each other. "Say, Timon," Pumbaa said, "this was quite a day for you. You've been a bird's mama and a kangaroo's kid. What are you going to be next? A monkey's uncle?"

Kanga the Brave

Written by Catherine McCafferty

Illustrated by Alvin S. White Studio

oo bounced out of bed, ready for adventure. Today, Roo decided, he would be Roo the Brave, Famous Explorer. He would find something really important in the deepest part of the Hundred-Acre Wood.

Roo the Brave hopped down the steps and swung open the front door. He was all set to dash out when his mother called, "Good morning, Roo, dear. Breakfast is ready."

"But, Mama," said Roo, "I'm going out for an explore. I don't have time for breakfast!"

Kanga just smiled and tapped the table. "A good breakfast will help you have a better explore," she said.

Roo the Brave frowned. Famous explorers shouldn't have to listen to their mothers, he thought. He dragged his feet all the way to the table, then started to gulp down his food.

"Don't gobble, Roo," said Kanga. "Take your time."

Roo tried to slow down, but he couldn't stop thinking about his explore. Finally, he finished his porridge and drank his milk. He hopped off his chair and raced to the door.

"Where are you going, dear?" asked Kanga.

"Into the woods, Mama," he said. He puffed out his chest. "I'm Roo the Brave!"

"The woods?" said Kanga. "Dear, I don't think that's such a good idea. Why don't we get the kite and— "

"Oh, Mama! Kites are for babies! I'm not a baby! I'm—"

"Roo the Brave." Kanga finished and smiled. "I know. But you're still my little Roo, too. Now, put on your scarf, and let me pack a lunch. I'll come with you."

41

Roo wound his scarf around his neck. No famous explorer ever took his mother along on a dangerous explore—especially not Roo the Brave! Roo was determined to have this adventure on his own. So before his mother had a chance to come back with his lunch, Roo raced out the door and into the woods.

"Tiiiiggggerrr! Tiiiiggggerrr!" Roo called. A moment later, Roo was bowled over by his bouncy friend.

"Say, Roo, what are you doing? Where's Mrs. Kanga?" Tigger put a hand above his eyes and looked around.

"Mama's letting me explore all by myself today," Roo said. He stood up as tall as he could. "I'm Roo the Brave, Famous Explorer. I'm going to find something really important in the deepest part of the woods." Roo thought for a minute. Every famous explorer had an explorer buddy. "Will you come with me, Tigger?" he asked.

"Hoo-hoo-hoo!" Tigger bounced around. "Tiggers love to explore. Say, what are we looking for, anyway?"

"Something important. I'll know when we find it!" Roo said, hopping with excitement.

Roo and Tigger bounced deeper and deeper into the Hundred-Acre Wood, farther and farther away from their homes. At first, the sun helped light up the woods. But after a while, the sun went behind some clouds. The sky grew dark, and the woods grew darker.

"Say, Roo," Tigger said. "Have we come to that 'something important' yet?"

Roo looked around. "I don't know," he muttered. "What we're looking for is in the deepest part of the woods."

Tigger picked up a stick and bounced a little ways forward, a little ways backward, a little ways to the left, and a little ways to the right. "Yep, by my calckerlations, we're in the deepest deep part."

Roo and Tigger stood still for a minute. The woods seemed very dark and quiet.

"I hope this isn't where the jagular hangs out," Tigger said.

Suddenly the sky turned dark. *BOOM!* The deafening sound made Roo and Tigger jump. *FLASH!* A bright bolt lit up the woods. "Um, Tigger," Roo whispered. "I don't know if I want to find the jagular."

"Well, I think you found 'im, Roo boy, but don't worry. We can outbounce 'im!" Tigger grabbed Roo's arm. They bounced off as fast as they could, dodging the old brown trees, which now looked like angry monsters to Tigger and Roo.

No matter which way they bounced, it seemed that the jagular was right behind them. Even to Roo the Brave, the thunder and lightning seemed like the growl of the jagular and the flash of his angry eyes. "Tigger, I'm s-s-scared," Roo said.

They stopped bouncing and looked around. Rain was coming down so hard that they couldn't see where they were, or where they were going.

"It's a good thing Tiggers never get lost," Roo said, looking up at Tigger hopefully.

"Er . . . Tiggers need to see where they're goin' so they can't get losted." Tigger scratched his head.

Just then another bright flash lit the forest. Roo and Tigger spotted a burrow under an old pine tree nearby.

"Let's wait under there," said Tigger. He pulled Roo into the burrow. Roo felt something yank on his scarf.

"The jagular's got me!" Roo yelped. He threw off his scarf and crawled as far into the burrow as he could.

"D-d-don't worry," Tigger said. "That big, old, fierce, scary jagular will never fit all the way under here . . . I hope."

The burrow was dry, but Tigger and Roo were soaked.
Water dripped down Roo's face, but he didn't mind. The
raindrops kept Tigger from seeing his teardrops.

The wind rattled the branches of the pine tree, and the thunder
boomed all around them. Roo the Brave wished he were Roo the
Home-in-Bed-With-Covers-Over-His-Head.

"I didn't even say good-bye to m-my mama," Roo said with a
sniff. "And now I'll never see her again."

"Don't worry, Roo," said Tigger. "Once this rain stops, your ol'
pal Tigger will get you home." With that, Tigger leaned back
against the side of the burrow and began to snore.

Roo leaned back against Tigger, but he was afraid to close his eyes. Tigger's snores helped drown out the booming. Then Roo heard another sound.

Oooooo! Ooooo!

Roo nudged Tigger awake. "Tigger, I think the jagular is still after us!" he whispered.

"Persistent fella, isn't he?" said Tigger.

The sound came closer. Tigger and Roo crawled farther into the burrow. Suddenly a light came toward them. Roo the Brave covered his eyes. He decided he didn't want to see a jagular, after all.

"Rooooo! There you are!" Kanga held up her lantern. "Mama!" Roo yelled. "How did you find us?"

Kanga pointed to Roo's scarf caught on a branch. "It's a good thing you took your scarf," she said with a smile.

Just then Roo heard an *Ooooo!* noise again. "The jagular!"

"It's all right, Roo," Kanga said.

There was a rush of wings, and then they heard a familiar voice. "I say, Roo," said Owl. "Did you find what you were looking for?"

Roo hugged his mother. "I sure did," he said. "I found Kanga the Brave, Famous Mama."

DISNEP
MICKEY MOUSE

MAID MINNIE AND THE EARL OF EDAM

Written by Liane Onish

Illustrated by Alvin S. White Studio

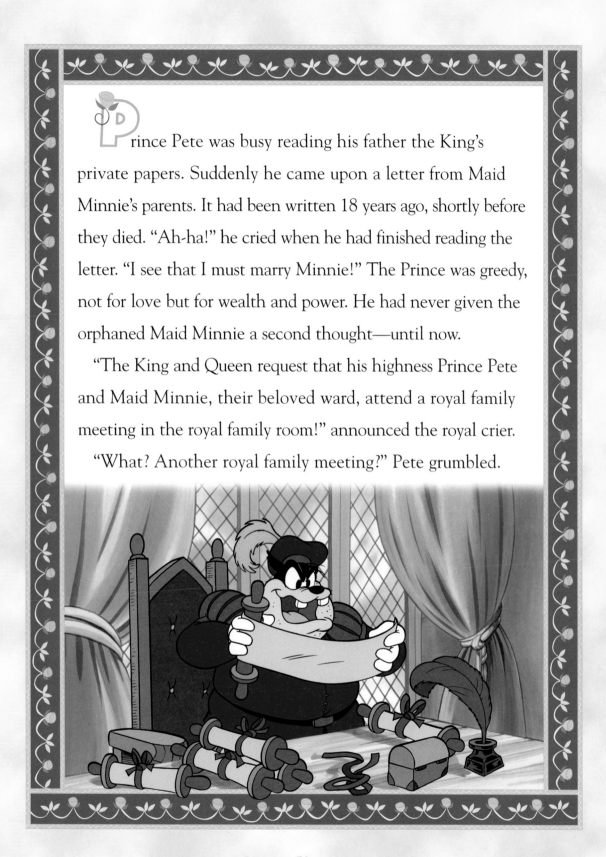

Prince Pete was busy reading his father the King's private papers. Suddenly he came upon a letter from Maid Minnie's parents. It had been written 18 years ago, shortly before they died. "Ah-ha!" he cried when he had finished reading the letter. "I see that I must marry Minnie!" The Prince was greedy, not for love but for wealth and power. He had never given the orphaned Maid Minnie a second thought—until now.

"The King and Queen request that his highness Prince Pete and Maid Minnie, their beloved ward, attend a royal family meeting in the royal family room!" announced the royal crier.

"What? Another royal family meeting?" Pete grumbled.

Maid Minnie had just returned from her morning ride. She dismounted and headed for the royal family room.

"How was your ride, my dear?" asked the Queen.

"Did you happen to meet Mickey, Earl of Edam, again?" guessed the King with a wink.

Maid Minnie blushed just as Prince Pete stomped in.

"The Queen and I have been invited to Bath to visit Lady Bubble and Sir Toyboat," the King announced. "And you, my son, will rule until we return."

Prince Pete smiled—a particularly nasty smile, Maid Minnie thought.

Outside the castle another meeting of sorts was taking place. "Come on, already!" squawked Friar Duck. Mickey sighed and followed his friend back to Edam.

"Why can't you fall in love with a princess? Someone with money?" Friar Duck complained. "Your castle turrets are leaking, your drawbridge is warped, and . . . "

But Mickey wasn't listening. He was daydreaming about his one true love—Maid Minnie.

Early the next morning, after the King and Queen had left for Bath, Maid Minnie saddled up for her daily ride. Much to her surprise, Prince Pete was in the stable.

"What a fine day! I shall ride with you," he said grandly.

"How . . . kind," she replied suspiciously.

When they were out of sight of the castle, the Prince smiled as sweetly as he could (which was not very) and said, "Maid Minnie, when shall we get married?"

Maid Minnie said, "When we find our one true love."

Prince Pete laughed. "You misunderstand me, my lady. By 'we,' I mean yourself, Maid Minnie—and me."

"But I don't love you," said Maid Minnie.

"Deep in my, er . . . heart, I have always loved you, dearest Minnie, although I may not have shown it," Pete assured her.

"I am sorry, Your Highness," Minnie said, "but my answer must be no."

Prince Pete was prepared for her refusal. He had another plan.

"So be it," he said. "Oh, I almost forgot—this letter came for you today."

"It's been opened!" she accused. The Prince just smiled.

"Dear Maid Minnie," Minnie read. "You must come to Bath. The Queen needs you. Signed, Lady Bubble."

"How odd," thought Maid Minnie.

Prince Pete was quite pleased with his forgery. Neither of them knew Lady Bubble or her handwriting.

"I'm sure she means for you to leave now," said the Prince, pretending to be concerned. Just then a carriage and two of the Prince's soldiers appeared. "Go. I shall send your things later."

Maid Minnie felt something was definitely not right. But she left anyway.

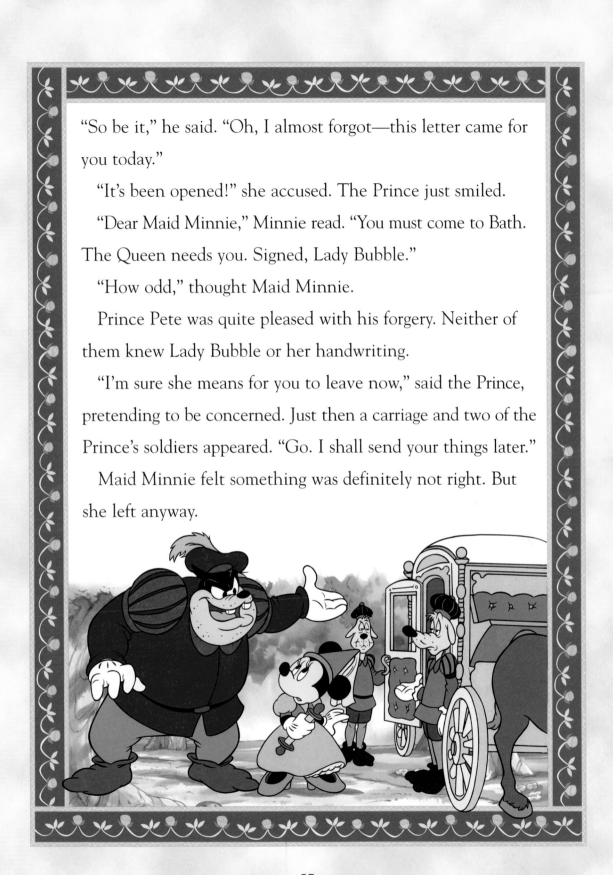

The Prince led Maid Minnie's horse back to the castle, smiling to himself. He knew that his soldiers would take Maid Minnie to his hunting lodge and keep her there.

As the Prince entered the castle, he pretended alarm. "Maid Minnie has been maid-napped!" he cried. "The bandits demand gold for her release! Send word throughout the kingdom: Triple taxes must be paid in gold, and at once!"

The castle was a flurry of activity. Messengers raced off with letters to all the lords in the kingdom. Prince Pete appeared upset, but inwardly he was extremely pleased with himself.

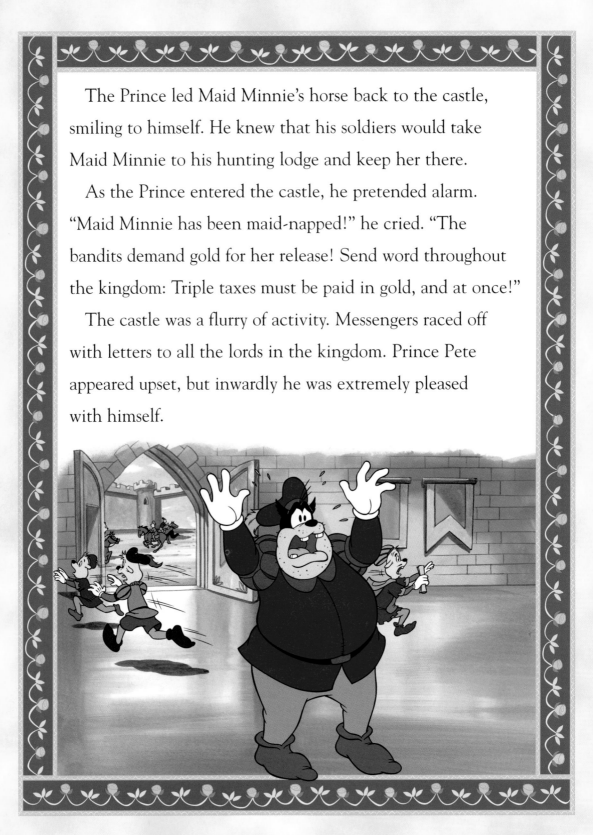

The carriage carrying Maid Minnie rushed past Sir Mickey without stopping. Thinking quickly, Minnie tossed her handkerchief out the window.

Sir Mickey picked it up. "Maid Minnie is in that carriage," he said. "Where is she going?" He turned his horse and galloped back to his own castle. Then he, Friar Duck, and a dozen soldiers set out after the carriage.

The fastest carriage was no match for soldiers on horseback. When the soldiers stopped the carriage, Maid Minnie quickly jumped out. "Oh, Sir Mickey!" she cried. "Something is not right. Prince Pete gave me a letter from Lady Bubble saying the Queen needs me in Bath. Why didn't the Queen write to me herself?"

Sir Mickey frowned. "The Queen did not write because she is not in Bath," he revealed. "The royal carriage broke down near Edam. The King and Queen are staying with *me* until their carriage is repaired."

Sir Mickey and Maid Minnie reached Edam castle just as the message from Prince Pete arrived. Friar Duck read it aloud: "Maid Minnie has been maid-napped! To pay her ransom, all taxes are hereby tripled and must be paid at once." The letter was signed King Pete.

"*King* Pete? Maid-napped? Ransom?" cried the King.

Maid Minnie said, "What can we do?"

"We'll storm the castle!" squawked Friar Duck.

"The Prince has many soldiers," the King pointed out.

"I have a plan," said Sir Mickey.

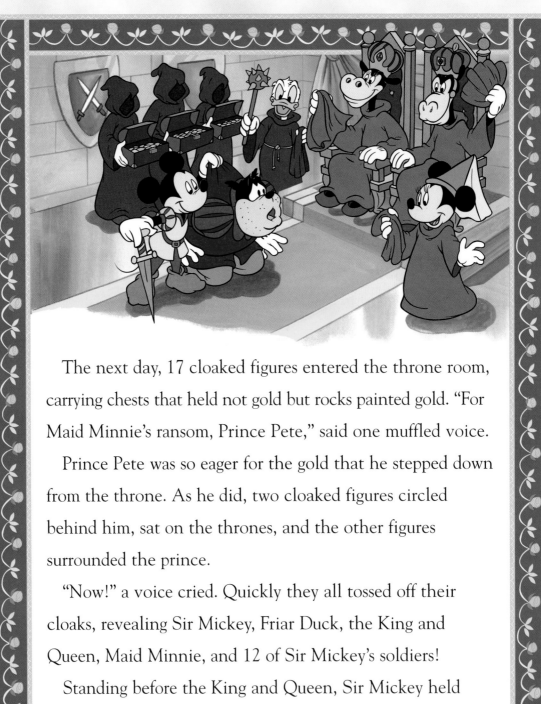

The next day, 17 cloaked figures entered the throne room, carrying chests that held not gold but rocks painted gold. "For Maid Minnie's ransom, Prince Pete," said one muffled voice.

Prince Pete was so eager for the gold that he stepped down from the throne. As he did, two cloaked figures circled behind him, sat on the thrones, and the other figures surrounded the prince.

"Now!" a voice cried. Quickly they all tossed off their cloaks, revealing Sir Mickey, Friar Duck, the King and Queen, Maid Minnie, and 12 of Sir Mickey's soldiers!

Standing before the King and Queen, Sir Mickey held Prince Pete at sword-point.

"Prince Pete, we strip you of your title," proclaimed the angry king. "You have lied, cheated, and maid-napped our dear Maid Minnie. You can no longer live in this kingdom. Henceforth you shall be called Plain Pete."

As Plain Pete was led away, the King turned toward Sir Mickey and said, "Name your reward, brave knight."

When Friar Duck heard the word *reward*, he perked up. He could think of a dozen things to ask for and turned to whisper to Sir Mickey, "The turrets are leaking, the drawbridge is warped. . . ."

"I want no reward, Sire," Sir Mickey said.

"Well, instead of a reward, would you accept gold and land as the dowry of your bride-to-be?" suggested the King.

Sir Mickey blushed. "No, Sire. Maid Minnie is the one and only true love of my life. I do not need a dowry."

The Queen smiled and said, "The dowry is Minnie's."

"What?" exclaimed Minnie and Mickey together.

The Queen explained. "When Minnie's parents died, they left her wealth and kingdom to us until she was of age. To keep her from fortune hunters, we kept her royalty a secret, even from her. We hoped she would find a husband who would lovingly care for her and her people. I believe Princess Minnie has found such a man."

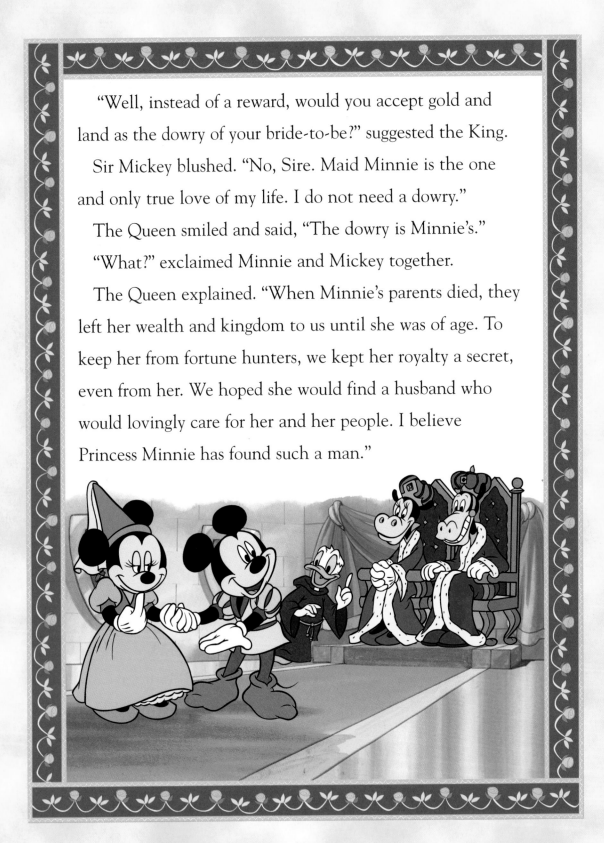

From that day on, Minnie was no longer known as Maid Minnie. She became Princess Minnie.

A week of wonderful wedding celebrations followed. Even Friar Duck was happy. And the leaking turrets and warped drawbridge of Edam castle were finally repaired.

101 DALMATIANS

PUPPY POWER

Written by Barbara Bazaldua

Illustrated by Alvin S. White Studio

One sunny spring morning, Roger marched into the
backyard of the new Dalmatian plantation. He was wearing a
big straw hat and carrying a shovel, rake, and hoe, as well as a
basket filled with seed packages, string, and planting sticks.

"I'm going to plant the biggest, greenest vegetable garden in
all of England!" he announced to the puppies, as they followed
him. "Just think, Patch—all the peas you can eat! Lucky shall
have lots of lettuce. And Rolly—why, you'll be munching
deeeelicious radishes from now until Christmas!"

"Yuck!" Rolly whispered. "Radishes don't sound 'deeeelicious' to me! Why doesn't he plant dog biscuits?"

Roger measured out the space for the garden. Then he began to dig.

"Let's help Roger!" Patch barked to the other puppies. They all began digging. Dirt and rocks flew through the air.

A pebble bounced off Roger's head.

"Whoa there, pups!" Roger said, rubbing his head and looking at the hole the puppies had dug. "We aren't digging a swimming pool. Better let me do it!"

The puppies sat down in the shade of a tree and watched Roger finish digging. Then he smoothed the earth. Next, he began putting sticks into the ground and tying string from one stick to another.

"Roger must want to play fetch," Lucky said to Penny. "Let's show him how good we are at fetching sticks." Penny and Lucky bounded into the garden, pulled up all the sticks and strings, and ran to Roger. Around and around his legs they ran, until his feet were completely tangled. Over he went, in a heap of puppies, sticks, and strings.

"No, no, puppies," Roger said, as he untangled himself. "We're not playing fetch today. Those sticks are to help me make straight rows for the seeds. Now, go sit down."

Once again, the pups trotted over to their shady spot and plopped down to watch.

"Look at Roger now!" Penny exclaimed. "He's burying something in the ground."

"Bones!" Rolly barked. "I bet he's burying bones." With a hungry little bark, Rolly followed Roger, digging up every hole that Roger had covered with dirt. But all he dug up were little round brown seeds. Rolly tasted a couple.

"Phooey!" Rolly spit them out. "Whatever these are, they taste *awful*!" he informed his brothers and sisters. "I hope they aren't radishes!"

Roger heard Rolly barking and turned around. Then he saw the holes. "Oh, gracious, puppies!" Roger exclaimed. "How will my garden grow with you digging? I'll have to find something for you to do."

Roger thought a moment. Then he gathered the puppies around him. He took a stick and drew a picture of a bird in the dirt.

"Now, this is a crow," Roger told the puppies. "Crows eat up all the seeds, so nothing can grow. I want you to watch the garden and chase off any crows you see. Can you do that?"

The puppies nodded their heads.

Roger drew another picture. "This is a rabbit, " he said. "They eat up all the plants. When you see one, I want you to bark loudly and chase it away. Can you do that?"

Once again, the puppies nodded.

So every day, the puppies watched Roger's garden. They barked at the crows and chased after the rabbits. At last, little green plants appeared in rows and began to grow taller and taller.

"Look how well my garden is growing," Roger said proudly. "You are excellent watch puppies!"

But what no one knew was that while the puppies were watching the garden every day, someone was watching them. Cruella De Vil had followed the puppies to the Dalmatian plantation, disguised in a long black coat and a big black hat.

"I'm not finished with those puppies yet," she muttered, swinging a long tan sack—just the right size to hold a couple of pups. "I'll watch and wait and wait and watch. Sooner or later, Roger and Anita will leave the plantation, and I'll nab those puppies."

Later that very afternoon, Roger and Anita went shopping. As they drove away, Cruella declared, "Now's my chance!"

73

Just as Cruella was sneaking up, Rolly spotted a rabbit.
"Woof! Scoot! Scram!" he barked, racing toward the little rabbit.
The other puppies joined in, chasing the rabbit up and down the
rows of vegetables. Then suddenly they heard a high cackling
laugh. The puppies froze. There stood Cruella, her long black
coat flapping around her like huge wings.

"It's a GIANT crow!" Rolly yelped.

"That's not a crow, it's CRUELLA!" Patch barked. "Run!"

Around and around the garden the puppies raced, with Cruella
after them. The confused little
rabbit ran this way and that,
looking for a way out.
Finally, with a frightened
squeak, the rabbit dashed
between Cruella's feet. . . .

Plop! Down went Cruella. *Clunk!* Down fell her long tan sack. *Splat!* Off flew her boots. *Whoosh!* Away flew her big back hat. Cruella's fall gave the puppies the time they needed.

"Dig! Dig! Dig a hole!" Rolly barked.

"Ooof! Uhh! Yahh!" Cruella shouted as pebbles and mud splatted, thunked, and plunked onto her head. "I'll get you yet!" she shouted, stumbling between the rows of cabbages and carrots.

"Some of you pups keep digging a deep hole," Rolly yelled. "The rest of you follow me. It's time to play fetch!"

Rolly raced for the sticks and strings and yanked them up. The other puppies followed him. Around and around they ran, winding the sticks and strings around Cruella's legs. Soon she was so tangled, she could barely move. As she yanked at the sticks and strings, her coat fell into the lettuce patch.

"You wretched dogs!" she screamed, lunging for Lucky.

At that moment the little rabbit dashed between her legs again. *Ker-plunk!* Cruella fell right into the very deep, very muddy hole that the puppies had dug.

"Aaah!" she screamed as she went down. "Arrgh!" she snarled as she struggled to stand, covered with mud.

Just then Roger and Anita returned from town. "What's going on?" Roger shouted.

Cruella turned and hopped out of the garden, across the field, and into the trees.

"Oh my! Look at my poor garden," Roger said, with a sigh. Then he looked at the puppies and smiled. "And look at all of you. You're all safe and sound, and that's what really counts."

Lucky trotted over, dragging Cruella's hat. Patch and Penny came carrying her boots and her sack. And Rolly dropped Cruella's long black coat at Roger's feet.

Roger looked at the clothes and began to laugh. "You're very good watch puppies," he said, "but now you'll have a little help. Let's use Cruella's long black coat and big black hat to make a scarecrow. We'll put her black boots on its feet, and hang her sack on its arm. What do you think of that?"

The puppies barked with glee. They had protected Roger's garden while he was gone, *and* they had gotten rid of the biggest pest of all—Cruella!

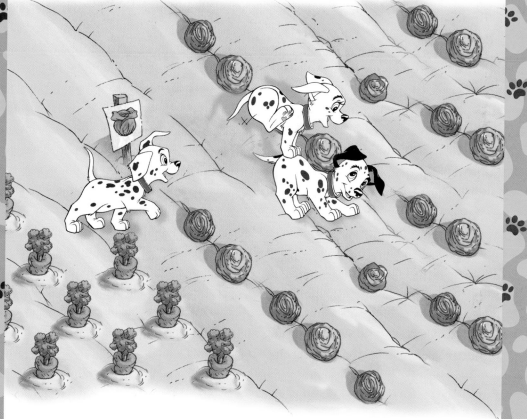

From then on, no crows or rabbits came anywhere near the garden. And soon Roger had the biggest, greenest garden in all of England.

POCAHONTAS

LITTLE BRAVE HEART

Written by Barbara Bazaldua

Illustrated by Alvin S. White Studio

"Nakoma, let's pick blackberries," Pocahontas suggested one hot summer day. "I found a patch full of ripe berries in a meadow up the river. We can go in my canoe."

"I love blackberries," Nakoma answered. "But should we go so far up the river without telling anyone?"

"Oh, we'll be back long before dark," Pocahontas answered, as they climbed into her canoe with Meeko and Flit. Meeko sat in the front of the canoe and splashed his paws in the water. Flit flew beside the canoe, as Nakoma and Pochontas paddled.

81

At last, they reached a small meadow beside the river. Pocahontas and Nakoma pulled the canoe onto a sandbar and walked into the meadow with Meeko and Flit close behind. The meadow was very pretty, with yellow and red flowers and deep green grass. On the other side of the meadow, a steep rocky slope rose up to high stone bluffs.

"My father said that one time it rained so hard that the river rose till it covered this meadow all the way to the bluffs," Pocahontas told her friends, as she led them to a blackberry patch covered with shiny, juicy berries.

Meeko immediately picked an armful of berries, then plumped right down and began stuffing them into his mouth with both paws.

Little Flit wanted to help Pocahontas. He tried to lift a berry basket, but it was too heavy. Then he tried to pick the berries and bring them to Pocahontas. But the prickly branches stuck to his wings.

"Oh, Flit, thank you for trying to help, but you're just too tiny," Pocahontas said gently, as she plucked the thorns from his wings.

Feeling very small and a little sad, Flit perched on a treetop alone. Below him, Pocahontas and Nakoma were singing as they picked berries. Meeko's tummy bulged as he stuffed berries into his mouth. Then suddenly a cold wind ruffled Flit's feathers. Flit looked at the sky and saw huge black storm clouds on the horizon.

Flit flew down to Pocahontas. "I can't play now, Flit," she said. "I'm busy picking berries." He tugged a strand of her hair to make her look at the sky. But Pocahontas brushed him away. "Stop teasing me, Flit," she said sternly.

But Flit couldn't give up. He knew it was dangerous to be caught in a big storm far from the village. He tugged at Pocahontas's dress, trying to pull her toward the canoe. But Pocahontas still wouldn't pay any attention. "We're not leaving until we've filled our baskets, Flit," she said.

Just then the wind blew the clouds over the sun. The sky grew dark. Thunder rumbled, and it began to rain.

As Meeko crawled beneath a berry basket to stay dry, Nakoma pointed toward the river. "Pocahontas, look," she cried, "the river!"

Pocahontas looked through the pouring rain. Nakoma was right. The river was beginning to churn over the riverbank and fill the meadow. As they watched, the canoe was carried away.

"What should we do?" Nakoma asked. "The river is rising so fast that it will soon flood the meadow."

"We must find shelter above the water!" Pocahontas replied. She looked around. But the rain was coming down so hard that she could barely see. "Flit, fly up and see if there is a place where we can all get out of the storm," Pocahontas called.

Flit struggled up through the rain and saw a small cave halfway up the bluffs. He flew back to Pocahontas, then darted toward the cave. "Flit has found a place for us," Pocahontas said. "Follow him!"

She picked up Meeko. Nakoma grabbed the full berry basket. They began to climb toward the cave. But the rocky ground was wet and slippery. With a cry, Nakoma slipped and fell, her foot twisted beneath her.

Pocahontas hurried to help her friend. "Oh no!" cried Nakoma. "I've hurt my ankle! I can't walk!"

"You can't lie here in the rain," said Pocahontas. "You must get up." She helped Nakoma stand. "Lean on me," Pocahontas said. Then she helped Nakoma limp toward the cave. Meeko and Flit went ahead of them. By the time they reached the cave, Nakoma was shaking from the cold, and her ankle was throbbing with pain.

"I must warm you, Nakoma," Pocahontas said. "But what can I use?" Flit noticed a pile of dried leaves and twigs the wind had blown inside the cave. He carried a leaf to Pocahontas.

"Oh, Flit," she said, "you've found just what I need to make a bed for Nakoma and a fire!"

Pocahontas quickly fixed a soft bed of dry leaves for Nakoma. Then Pocahontas made another pile of leaves and twigs. Next she took a flintstone from the leather pouch at her waist.

"I will use the stone to strike a spark onto these leaves," she told Flit. "Fan the spark with your wings until it becomes a flame." Flit did as Pocahontas asked. In a few minutes, a cozy fire was warming the chilly cave.

"Now, if I only had some comfrey leaves to put on your ankle to stop the swelling," Pocahontas told Nakoma.

Flit remembered seeing some comfrey plants on the bluffs above the cave. He flew up, broke off two large leaves, and carried them to the cave.

"Thank you, Flit," Pocahontas said when she saw the leaves. She wrapped them around Nakoma's ankle and found a thong in her pouch to secure them.

"My ankle feels better already," Nakoma said.

Outside, the rain poured down. "Our families will be very worried," Pocahontas told Flit and Meeko, "and Nakoma should not stay in this cave too long, or she will become ill. But without my canoe, I can't go to the village for help. I don't know what to do."

Flit looked at the rain. He looked at the rising river. He knew he could fly across it and reach the village. Even though he was already wet and cold, Flit zipped out of the cave.

"Flit, come back!" Pocahontas called. But Flit could not turn back. The wind tossed him up and pushed him down. The rain soaked his wings and beat on his head. But Flit flew on. Thunder rumbled. Lightning flashed. The river roared and churned. But Flit kept on through the storm to the village.

Back at the cave, Pocahontas and her friends waited. Nakoma fell asleep on her leaf bed by the fire. Meeko ate all the berries. Pocahontas fed twigs to the fire and thought about Flit's journey. "I hope he's safe," she thought. "He's so small, and the storm is so big!"

At last, the thunder and lightning faded. As Pocahontas looked out, the sun broke through the clouds, and a beautiful rainbow appeared over the flooded meadow.

Then Pocahontas saw the most beautiful sight of all.
Up the river came a row of canoes. Her father, Chief
Powhatan, was in the lead canoe. And in front of him, a
tiny figure flashed brightly in the sun's rays. "It's Flit!"
Pocahontas called to Meeko and Nakoma. "He's leading
my father to us!"

The canoes paddled across the flooded meadow to the
bluffs. Chief Powhatan and the warriors stepped from
the canoes and followed Flit up to the cave.

The Chief and the other warriors carefully carried
Nakoma to the canoes. Pocahontas, Meeko, and Flit
followed closely behind.

"Nakoma's ankle will mend well," Powhatan told his daughter. "You have taken good care of her."

"Thank you, Father," Pocahontas answered. "But Flit has taken the best care of us."

"It is true," Powhatan replied smiling. "He flew through the storm to lead us to you. Your tiny friend is very brave."

Flit perched on Pocahontas's shoulder. Pocahontas stroked him gently. "I will tell a story in the longhouse on feast days about how you saved us," she told him. "And in the story, I will give you a second name," Pocahontas continued. "You will always be Flit to me. But from now on, every time your story is told, you will be called Little Brave Heart."